TEN NIGHTS
DREAMING
AND THE CAT'S GRAVE

Natsume Sōseki

A New English Translation by
Matt Treyvaud

Foreword by Michael Emmerich

Introduction by Susan Napier

DOVER PUBLICATIONS, INC.
Mineola, New York

Bibliographical Note

Ten Nights Dreaming, first published by Dover Publications, Inc., in 2015, is a newly translated edition of the work originally serialized in Japanese in the *Asahi Shimbun* in 1908; the story "The Cat's Grave" is also included in this edition. Written specially for this edition are a Translator's Note by Matt Treyvaud; a Foreword by Michael Emmerich; and an Introduction by Susan Napier.

International Standard Book Number

ISBN-13: 978-0-486-79703-8
ISBN-10: 0-486-79703-1

Manufactured in the United States by LSC Communications
79703104   2023
www.doverpublications.com

Contents

TRANSLATOR'S NOTE

These translations are based on the Aozora Bunko texts of *Yume jūya* and *Eijitsu shōhin*, accessible online via **www.aozora.gr.jp**. Reference was also made to two other versions of *Ten Nights Dreaming*: the text contained in *Sōseki kinjū shihen* ("Four recent works by Sōseki"), published in 1910 by Shunyōdō and accessible online through the National Diet Library's website; and the text in Iwanami Shoten's most recent *Sōseki zenshū* ("Complete works of Sōseki"), published from 1993 to 1999. The commentary in Sasabuchi Tomoichi's *"Yume jūya" ron hoka* ("On 'Ten Nights Dreaming' and other topics"), published by Meiji Shoin in 1986, also proved particularly valuable.

Since the unusual character of *Ten Nights Dreaming* lies not only in story but also in technique, this translation attempts to recreate the structure and flow of the original as closely as possible without becoming pedantic and unreadable. Where Sōseki uses multiple methods to indicate dialogue, for example, this is reflected in the translation. Japanese terminology is also retained where there is no sufficiently equivalent word in English, notably in reference to material culture such as clothing and architecture. The first instance of each such Japanese terminology has been footnoted with an explanation.

The italicized notes at the beginning of each dream do not correspond to anything in the source text. Rather, they have been added as a compromise to help provide readers with enough basic background knowledge to appreciate each part of the work on its own terms.

Matt Treyvaud
Shōnan, 2015

FOREWORD

I can't recall when I first read *Ten Nights Dreaming*. Yet the experience of reading it comes to me with an almost unnerving clarity, as vividly as a scent summoned by something in the wind, without warning, from some ordinarily inaccessible substratum of memory. It could have been a decade ago, maybe even longer. I know I read it in Japanese, but in what edition? Was I in Kyoto, New York, Tokyo?

Certain literary masterpieces have this effect: the impression they create is so intense, so unique, that it overloads our senses, preventing us from registering the context within which we encounter them. Our brains record the feelings they evoke in us less as a discrete memory than as a category of experience, less an event than a mood. For me, *Ten Nights Dreaming* is this kind of masterpiece.

Recognizing the special power of these books is not as easy as one might think. Just as some cue is needed to summon the memory of that scent, so too it takes a second, entirely different book, encountered in a different place and time, to make us see how deep and distinctive an impression the first has made upon us. It takes, that is to say, a masterful translation. For me, Matt Treyvaud's *Ten Nights Dreaming* is just such a translation. Reading it, I found myself being drawn once again into the distinctive, uncanny mood this book first created in me all those years ago.

When they recount their dreams, people often describe feeling as though they had been in that precise scene or landscape before. That sense of déjà vu, more than anything, stands at the core of my memory of first reading *Ten Nights Dreaming*. I can think of no better way to express my admiration for what Matt Treyvaud has accomplished in this book than to say I felt that same déjà vu all over again in reading this translation.

Michael Emmerich
May 2015

INTRODUCTION

"Dreams are the royal road to the unconscious," proclaimed Sigmund Freud, suggesting that we find hidden aspects of ourselves through dreaming. But in the case of Natsume Sōseki's beautiful and eerie fantasy collection *Ten Nights Dreaming*, we might perhaps ask, "Whose unconscious do you mean?" Is it Sōseki the writer's unconscious? Or is it the collective unconscious of Japan at a crossroads moment in its history? Or could it even be the reader's own unconscious, because this collection of dreams stirs and provokes us in complex and memorable ways each time we read it?

In fact, all of the above probably are true. Reading *Ten Nights Dreaming* we gain access to the many-layered mind and imagination of Sōseki, one of modern Japan's greatest—and most anguished—writers. And we also gain entry into the uneasy, multifaceted world of Japan during the Meiji period (1868–1912), a time when Japan pulled and pushed itself out of a tradition-bound feudal society to confront the challenge of modernity brought on by its recent contact with the West. Sōseki's concerns were not merely culturally specific, however: Most of the anxieties and challenges he chronicles are universally experienced by modern human beings, and the strange, uneasy dreams he recounts flicker and resound across our own brains even a hundred years later.

It is little wonder that issues of identity abound throughout the dreams. Mirrors, a hat, blindness, and a shadowy sinister child appear, signifiers of the self or at least of the search for the self. These images relate both to Sōseki's own personal and aesthetic experiences and to the deep transitions convulsing his country as a whole. Later on Sōseki would write about these issues in a number of realistic novels for which he is most famous, but in many ways the fantastic, grotesque, and occasionally lyrical imagery in *Ten Nights Dreaming* and other early fantasy works expresses these concerns in more profound and memorable ways. The fantastic, as scholars and psychologists from Bruno Bettelheim onwards have reminded us, can be an extremely effective method of processing traumatic issues in a safely displaced fashion. By [dis]placing our deepest fears, anxieties, or hopes into the realm of the fantastic, we can work through them at a secure psychological distance, removed from the sometimes too painful directness of realistic fiction or art.

Certainly, Sōseki had ample reasons for using the fantastic mode to work through trauma. His life contained a number of traumatic events, beginning in his infancy. Sōseki was born in 1867 to aged parents who, embarrassed to have a child at an advanced age, farmed him out to another couple. When he later returned to his parents, they pretended for a while that they were his grandparents, and he only learned the truth through a late-night whisper from a kindly maid. Fortunately for Sōseki, he escaped his unhappy household through his brilliance as a student, first mastering Chinese and then going on to become one of a handful of Japanese students to become truly literate in English literature.

Sōseki's success in English, however, led to one of the most traumatic periods in his life, a two-year stint in London arranged by the Japanese government. Although he arrived boasting that he would out-master the English in their own language, he soon realized that his spoken English would never achieve fluency. As all his biographers chronicle, these two years were the most miserable in Sōseki's life. By his own account he lived "like a stray dog among wolves," lonely and fearful, ashamed of his own failure and resentful of the English. The dream of "The Seventh Night," with its vision of an alienated Japanese man on a ship full of Westerners steadily moving towards the setting sun, undoubtedly expresses the disturbing, even despairing, emotions that Sōseki felt towards his own encounter with the West.

But it is also true that his time in England provided Sōseki with some of his most memorable and beautiful material for his early fantastic literature. Visits to the Tower of London not only gave him the inspiration to write the ghostly tale "The Tower of London," but also may have inspired the themes of claustrophobia or outright entrapment evident in the dreams of the second, fifth, and tenth nights. "Tower" also deals with the inescapable power of a dark past that still shadows the present, a theme that appears as the climax of the dream of "The Third Night," widely acknowledged to be the most gripping and haunting of all the dreams.

More positive inspirations from Sōseki's time in London also exist and are at least as important as the dark shadows of the Tower. Most significant were his visits to the Tate Gallery in London and his encounters with the poetry and art of the Pre-Raphaelites and the Arthurian poetry of Alfred, Lord Tennyson. Both Tennyson and the Pre-Raphaelites looked back to a premodern world of beauty, grace, and chivalry often embodied in the figure of a beautiful, and sometimes dying, woman. Sōseki apparently spent many hours at the Tate transfixed in front of John William Waterhouse's picture of the Lady of Shalott, the legendary lover of Lancelot who died tragically (and beautifully) of unrequited love. The Lady and her Arthurian equivalent, Elaine, were both associated with lilies, and it is easy to see another incarnation of her in Sōseki's flower-woman of the lyrical "Dream of the First Night."

"The First Night" also contains an image of entrapment, but in this case the male observer seems content to stay spellbound by the woman's power. In "The Second Night," the male is imprisoned by his own ego, although there may be a hidden sexual element as well, given his references to his "nine and a half inch knife." Sexuality and entrapment reach a crescendo in the grotesque black humor of the dream of the "Tenth Night," in which a mysterious woman leads "Shotaro" (perhaps the dreamer's alter ego) to a hideous fate of being charged by an endless stream of pigs and then licked by one. It seems that all that will be left of Shotaro is his beloved Panama hat, a last fragmented image of identity. Critics have long known that Sōseki's own marriage was an unhappy one, and these conflicting images of beauty and entrapment are suggestive of his psychological state at that time.

But the image of a pure and dying woman etched in "The First Night" may have larger cultural references as well, suggesting a general need among modernizing nations for an image of organic purity and beauty removed, at least momentarily, from the taint of industrialization. Across cultures this image is often embodied in the vision of a dying or vanishing woman, and it is perhaps not surprising that Sōseki returns to this image in his later realistic novel *And Then,* and in his last, unfinished novel, *Light and Dark.*

The popularity of these later novels with his contemporary Japanese audience attests that Sōseki's work struck a major chord in the hearts of the citizens of the Meiji period. His later work was famous for its themes concerning the increase in isolated egotistical individuals, the relentlessness and bewildering quality of technological progress, and the disappearance of faith. All these themes appear in the earlier *Ten Nights Dreaming.* We have already mentioned the dream of "The Seventh Night," with its vision of a ship and its alienated passengers steaming relentlessly toward an unknown future, a metaphor for Meiji Japan as much as for the dreamer himself. The relentless vision of the final dream with its nonstop stream of pigs goes beyond issues of sexual insecurity to hint at a deep unease with progress in and of itself. Similarly, the dream of the "Eighth Night" limning a busy barbershop in which the protagonist attempts to change his appearance as he gazes at the reflections of passersby in a mirror suggests the crazy pace and insecurities of the newly modern world.

The dreams of the second, fifth, sixth, and ninth nights depict their protagonists' attempts to believe in something beyond themselves, only to end up frustrated or betrayed. The woman in the dream of "The Ninth Night" prays to a god to help her samurai husband, not realizing that he is already dead. The old man in "The Fifth Night," perhaps a Taoist immortal, seems unable to wield his magic, and, similar to the dreamer in "The Seventh Night," ends up disappearing beneath the surface of the water. Most poignant of all is the dream of "The Sixth Night," in which a sculptor of the Meiji period attempts to summon medieval "Benevolent Kings" from the wood of modern logs, only to ruefully conclude that "Benevolent Kings simply were not buried in Meiji trees," a resigned acknowledgment of the absence and emptiness that signify the modern world.

Sōseki wrote *Ten Nights Dreaming* three years after his return from London and two years after the publication of his first major work, the satirical and somewhat fantastical *I Am a Cat*, the story of a Meiji household told from a cat's point of view. The somber little piece "The Cat's Grave," which ends the present collection, is told in entirely realistic terms, giving the reader a hint of Sōseki's later fiction. The piece acts as a bridge between his fantastic pieces and his realistic fiction, since it concerns the very real death of a previously fantastical cat.

At the same time, the story's placement in this collection also reminds the reader of the power of dreams and fantasy. A realistic account of a cat's death and burial memorializes a specific cat at a specific time and place. Compare this with the death and burial that provide the framework of the story in the dream of

"The First Night," which begins this collection. It is up to the reader to use his or her imagination to play with the image of a fragment of a star worn round "through its long passage through the sky" or the vision of a woman transforming into a flower for a final kiss. These images reach into our unconscious, opening up roads and realms beyond ourselves and inspiring, perhaps, our own dreams, be they lyrical, grotesque, terrifying, or, as with Sōseki's dreams, all of the above.

Susan Napier
April 2015

TEN NIGHTS DREAMING
AND THE CAT'S GRAVE

The First Night

The First Night

*The first dream is a relatively straightforward tale whose vivid
imagery foreshadows many of the themes running
through the collection.*

This is what I dreamed.

I was sitting, arms folded, by the pillow of a woman who
lay with her face towards the sky. ——I am dying, she said in a
quiet voice. Her long, flowing hair spread across her pillow,
framing the soft outlines of her oval face. Within the pure white
of her cheeks her blood showed its color warmly, and her lips,
of course, were red. She did not look about to die at all. But she
had said quite distinctly, in her quiet voice, that she was dying.
I found myself in agreement with her: she would surely die.
——Are you sure? Are you really dying? I asked, peering down
at her face. Her eyes opened wide. ——Yes, she replied. I am
dying. Within the long lashes that enclosed her large, moist eyes
was the purest black. In the depths of those pure black pupils
my form floated vivid and clear.

Gazing at those shining dark eyes, so deep that they were
almost transparent, I could not accept that she would die.
Lowering my mouth to her pillow, I spoke again. ——You
aren't dying, surely. You'll be fine, I said. You'll be fine.
——No, I am dying, the woman insisted in the same small

1

voice, eyes drowsy but not yet closed. There's nothing to be done about it.

——Well, can you see my face? I asked, watching her closely.

——Why, she replied with a smile, Isn't that its reflection, right there? I straightened up again in silence. Folding my arms, I wondered if she really had to die.

Some time later, the woman spoke again.

"When I am dead, please bury me. Dig a hole with a large oyster shell. Then use a fallen fragment from a star to mark where I lie. That done, please wait beside the grave. I will come to you again."

I asked her when that would be.

"The sun will rise, as you know. After that, it will set. Then it will rise again, and then set again. Can you wait for me, even as the red sun[1] sinks from east to west, east to west?"

I nodded silently.

A new note of determination entered the woman's quiet voice. "Please wait a hundred years," she said. "Sit beside my grave and wait a hundred years. I will come to you, I promise."

I told her simply that I would wait. At once, I saw my form in her black eyes, so vivid and clear, begin to blur and break. Just as it started to run, like a reflection in still water muddled by movement, the woman shut her eyes tightly. A tear spilled from between her eyelashes onto her cheek. She was dead.

I went down to the garden and dug a hole with an oyster shell. The shell was sharp, with a long, gently curved edge. The mother-of-pearl inside the shell glinted in the moonlight with every scoop of earth I removed. The smell of damp earth was in the air too. After a time the hole was complete. I lowered the woman into it. Then I gently covered her with the soft earth.

---

1. **Red sun:** Traditionally, in Japan the sun is described as red rather than yellow.

The mother-of-pearl inside the shell caught the moonlight with each scoop.

This done, I went and found a fallen fragment from a star to place on top. The fragment was round. I supposed that its corners had been worn away during its long fall through the sky, leaving it smooth. I felt the warmth of the fragment against my breast and in my hands as I cradled it in both arms and lowered it carefully into place.

I sat down on some moss. *So this is how I will spend the next hundred years*, I thought, gazing at the round gravestone with my arms crossed. Before long, the sun rose in the east, just as the woman had said it would. It was a large, red sun. Eventually, again just as the woman had said, the sun set in the west. It stayed as red as ever as it sank out of sight. *One*, I counted.

Some time later the crimson orb slowly rose again. Then it silently sank. *Two*, I counted again.

I do not know how many such suns I counted. I counted and counted, but more passed overhead than I could possibly count. And yet a hundred years had still not passed. Finally, staring at the round stone, which was by now covered with moss, I began to wonder if the woman had not deceived me.

At that moment a green shoot appeared from under the stone, stretching up towards me at an angle as it grew. The shoot grew longer as I watched, stopping just as it reached my chest. Then, as the shoot swayed from side to side, the single long, thin bud at its drooping tip softly opened its petals. It was a pure white lily[2] right under my nose, so fragrant that I felt it in my bones. A single dewdrop fell onto it from far above, making the lily rock back and forth under its own weight. I leaned forward and kissed its cold, white, dew-moistened petals. As I straight-

---

2. **Lily:** The Japanese word for "lily" is written with two characters that mean "hundred" and "meet."

ened up again, I happened to see the dawn star twinkling all alone in the distant sky.

I realized then for the first time that a hundred years had passed.

The Second Night

The Second Night

In the second dream, the narrator finds himself a samurai in a Zen temple. Perhaps drawing on his own experiences at Engaku-ji temple in the 1890s, Sōseki distorts the imagery and rhetoric of Zen to portray a fundamental misapprehension of the nature of Zen practice.

This is what I dreamed.

Leaving the *oshō's*[1] room, I followed the corridor back to my own and found the *andō*[2] burning dully. When I half-knelt on a cushion to adjust the wick, the charred tip broke off and tumbled like a flower to the red lacquered stand below. At the same time, the room brightened.

The picture on the *fusuma*[3] was a Buson.[4] Black willows were drawn densely here and sparsely there below a shivering fisherman traversing an embankment, woven *kasa*[5] askew. The alcove was hung with a scroll depicting Mañjuśrī crossing the

---

1. **Oshō:** The head priest of a Zen temple.
2. **Andō:** A wooden-framed paper lamp.
3. **Fusuma:** Sliding rectangular room dividers.
4. **Buson:** Yosa Buson (1716–1783), one of Japan's greatest haiku poets and artists.
5. **Kasa:** A conical woven hat worn to keep off the sun and rain.

sea.[6] The fragrance of incense lingered in the room's dimmer reaches. The temple was so large and still that it felt deserted. When I glanced up at the black ceiling, for a moment the pool of shadow cast there by the round *andō* looked like a living thing.

Still on one knee, I turned up a corner of the cushion with my left hand and reached underneath with my right. There it was, just as it should be. Thus reassured, I let the corner fall back into place and sat down on the cushion heavily.

——You are a samurai, the *oshō* had said. As a samurai, *satori*[7] should not be beyond you. Watching you sit there, day after day, with no *satori* to show for it — well, perhaps you are no samurai after all. Human garbage would be more like it! Oho, now you are angry, he had continued with a laugh. If what I say upsets you, then find *satori* and bring me proof. With that, he had turned his face away. The insolence!

I would show him. I would reach *satori* before the clock in the alcove one room over struck the next hour. Having done so, I would return for a second interview with him that very night. And at that interview I would exchange my *satori* for his head. I could not take his life without achieving *satori* first. There was no option but to succeed. I was a samurai.

If *satori* proved beyond me, I would turn my blade on myself. No samurai can live in humiliation. I would die quickly and cleanly.

At this thought, I found my hand slipping under the cushion again. When it came out, it was holding a *tantō*[8] in a red lac-

---

6. **Mañjuśrī crossing the sea:** A depiction of Mañjuśrī, bodhisattva of wisdom in East Asian Buddhism, crossing the ocean with his attendants to arrive in Japan.

7. **Satori:** A technical term in Zen Buddhism often translated "enlightenment" or "realization."

8. **Tantō:** A short, dagger-like sword, usually less than a foot in length.

quered scabbard. I grasped the sword by the hilt. The cold blade gleamed once in the dark room as I cast the scabbard aside. Something terrible seemed to stream from my hand, gathering to a single point of murderous intent at the tip of the blade. Seeing the wicked blade mercilessly reduced to a pinprick, driven to a sharpening point at the end of its full nine and a half inches, I felt a sudden urge to drive it deep. All the blood in my body flowed towards my right wrist, and the hilt felt sticky in my grip. My lips trembled.

Returned the *tantō* to its scabbard and placing it close to me on my right, I crossed my legs into the full lotus position. Jōshū said, "*mu*."[9] But what was "*mu*" supposed to mean? Pious jackass! I gritted my teeth.

My back teeth ground together so fiercely that my breath came hot and ragged through my nose. There was a painful tightness at my temples. I forced my eyes open twice as wide as usual.

I saw the scroll. I saw the *andō*. I saw the *tatami*.[10] I saw the *oshō*'s great bald kettle of a head as clearly if it were right in front of me. I even heard the mocking laugh from his crocodilian mouth. Insolent, bald-headed fool! There was no way around it: that kettle had to come off his shoulders. I would attain this satori of his. *Mu, mu*! I strained at the word from the root of my tongue. But for all my *mu*s, I still smelled incense. How dare mere incense interfere!

---

9. **Jōshū said, "*mu*.":** A reference to "Jōshū's dog," the first *kōan* in the thirteenth-century collection known in Japanese as *Mumonkan* (often translated as "The Gateless Gate" in English). The full *kōan* as given in the *Mumonkan* is: "A monk asked Jōshū, 'Does a dog have Buddha-nature?' Jōshū replied, '*Mu*.'" Jōshū was a Chinese Zen master, and *mu* is the Japanese pronunciation of a Chinese word whose meaning here has been interpreted as everything from an inexpressible nothingness to a simple "No." Mumon Ekai, compiler of the Mumonkan, called Jōshū's "*Mu*" the gate through which all those seeking enlightenment must pass.

10. **Tatami:** Woven, stuffed mats used for flooring.

I suddenly clenched my fists and battered my head until it hurt. I ground my teeth back and forth. Sweat ran down my sides. My back was stiff as a wooden pole. My knee joints flared with pain. Let them break, then, I thought, but it still hurt. It was excruciating. *Mu* was yet to make its appearance. Every time it seemed on the verge of appearing, the pain returned. It was enraging. It was mortifying. I was humiliated beyond belief. Tears rolled down my cheeks. I longed for some great boulder I could hurl myself against, dashing body and bone alike to pieces.

And yet I endured, seated and still. An unbearable despair swelled in my breast. It seized me bodily from below and rushed through me, desperately seeking escape through my pores, but every surface was blocked; it was trapped with no exit in the cruelest of circumstances.

My mind began to warp. The *andō* and the Buson, the *tatami* mats and the overlapping shelves — all were there and not there, not there yet there. But still there was no sign of *mu*. It seemed that I had just been sitting around to no particular purpose And then, without warning, the clock in the next room began to chime.

I started. My right hand went straight to the *tantō*. The clock chimed a second time.

The Third Night

The Third Night

In the third dream, the series takes a turn for the sinister. Some see a connection between the events of this dream and Sōseki's own unhappy childhood.

This is what I dreamed.

I was carrying a child of almost six on my back. It was clear to me that he was my son. Mysteriously, however, he had gone blind at some point, and his head was shaved blue. ——When did you go blind? I asked him, and he replied, ——What? I've been blind forever. His voice was unmistakably a child's, but he spoke just like an adult. As an equal, in fact.

Green rice paddies lay to the left and right. The path was narrow. From time to time a heron's form flashed in the gloom.

"We've reached the paddies, then," the child on my back said.

"How did you know?" I asked, twisting around to see him.

"The herons — can't you hear them calling?" he asked.

At this a heron did indeed let out two short cries.

I was beginning to fear this child, son of mine though he be. Who knew what lay in store for me, carrying something like him on my back? Wondering if there was somewhere I could dump him, I saw a large forest in the darkness that lay ahead. No sooner had I thought *That might do it* than I heard a chuckle from my back.

13

"What's so funny?" I asked.

The child did not answer me. "Am I heavy, Father?" he asked.

"No," I replied. "You're not heavy."

"I will be," he said.

Keeping the forest in sight, I walked on in silence. The path through the paddies was irregular and winding, never quite leading where I wanted to go. Finally we arrived at a fork in the road. I paused for a moment right where the roads parted to catch my breath.

"There should be a stone marker," the boy said.

Just as he said, a small pillar of stone stood nearby, eight inches square and as tall as my waist. According to the pillar, the left fork led to Higakubo and the right to Hottahara.[1] Dark as it had gotten, the red lettering was clearly visible. The characters were the same red as a newt's belly.

"You'll want to go left," the boy ordered. Looking left I saw the forest from before rising into the sky, casting its dark shadow down over our heads. I hesitated.

"Don't hold back on my account," the boy said. Seeing nothing else for it, I began walking towards the forest. There were no more forks in the path now. *Sure knows a lot for a blind kid,* I thought to myself as we drew near the forest, and then heard the voice from my back again: "I know it makes things difficult, my being blind."

"I'm carrying you, aren't I? What's the problem?"

"I appreciate that, but I won't put up with mockery. Especially from my own father."

I couldn't stand any more of this. I quickened my pace to get to the forest and dump him as soon as I could.

---

1. **Higakubo and ... Hottahara:** Actual place names in the Tokyo of Sōseki's day.

"You'll understand a little further on," the boy said from my back. Then he spoke again, as if talking to himself. "It was an evening just like this, come to think of it."

"What was?" I asked, strain in my voice.

"'What was'!" the child sneered. "As if you didn't know!" And with this I began to feel as if I did know, somehow. I couldn't quite put my finger on what had happened, but I was sure it had been an evening just like this one. I also felt that I would, indeed, understand a little further on — and that this understanding would be a terrible thing, so it was imperative that I dump the boy, quickly, before it could arrive. I walked even faster.

It had been raining for a while now. The path grew darker by degrees. But the little boy clinging to my back shone like a mirror from which nothing escaped, casting a merciless light on every part of my past, present and future. What's more, this boy was my own son. And blind, at that. It was unbearable.

"This is the place, right here. Right at the root of that cedar."

I heard the boy's voice clearly through the rain. Before I knew what I was doing, I had stopped. We had entered the forest at some point. The black thing a few paces ahead, I had to admit, looked like a cedar tree, just as the boy said.

"It was at the root of that cedar, wasn't it, Father?"

"Yes," I replied, without thinking. "It was."

"The fifth year of Bunka — the Year of the Dragon."[2]

Fifth year of Bunka, Year of the Dragon: this sounded right to me.

"It was exactly a hundred years ago that you killed me."

As soon as I heard these words, the knowledge burst into my head: one hundred years ago, in the fifth year of Bunka — the

---

2. **Fifth year of Bunka–Year of the Dragon:** This corresponds to 1808 on the Gregorian calendar, precisely 100 years before the publication of *Ten Nights Dreaming*.

year of the dragon — on a dark evening just like this, I had killed a blind man at the root of this very cedar tree. *I'm a murderer,* I realized at last, and as it hit me the child on my back was suddenly as heavy as a roadside statue of Jizō.[3]

---

3. **Roadside statue of Jizō:** "Jizō" is the Sino-Japanese name for the bodhisattva Kṣitigarbha. In Japan, Jizō is revered as a guardian of children, particularly those who die before their parents, and statues of Jizō can commonly be found by the roadside and in cemeteries.

The Fourth Night

The Fourth Night

The central figure of the fourth dream, as Sasabuchi Tomoichi points out, appears to be a cross between a Taoist immortal and a Meiji street peddler.

In the middle of a large room with a floor of pounded earth stood something like a bench surrounded by little folding stools. The bench was a glossy black in color. An old man sat drinking by himself in the corner at a square *zen* tray[1] with a small dish of *nishime* stew[2] on it.

The old man was already quite ruddy with drink. Beyond that, his face positively shone with vitality, without even a wrinkle. The only thing that revealed his age was his long white beard. Still a child myself, I wondered just how old he might be. Then the proprietress came in, wiping her hands on her apron and carrying a small wooden bucket which she must have just filled with water at the bamboo *kakei*[3] out back.

"How old are you, *ojii-san*?"[4] she asked.

---

1. **Zen tray:** A lacquered square tray on legs used for serving food.

2. **Nishime stew:** A dish of stewed vegetables, usually including sweet potato, carrot, and other root vegetables along with *shiitake* mushrooms, *konnyaku* (yam cake) and *kombu* kelp.

3. **Kakei:** A bamboo water spout placed at the edge of a pond to create a fountain.

4. **Ojii-san:** Literally, "grandfather," but usable in certain circumstances to address unrelated men of an advanced age.

The old man's cheeks were bulging with food, and he had to swallow before he could reply. "I can't remember," he said at last.

The proprietress tucked her hands into her narrow *obi*[5] and stood where she was, looking across at the old man's face. The old man threw back a mouthful of sake from a large cup that looked like a rice bowl and then let out a long, audible exhalation through his white beard. As he did, the proprietress spoke again. "Where do you live?" she asked.

The old man cut his exhalation short. "Inside my navel," he said.

"And where are you headed?" asked the proprietress, hands still in her narrow *obi*.

The old man drained his cup again and let out another long breath before replying. "I'm going away," he said.

"Straight ahead?" asked the proprietress. As she spoke, the old man's breath went through the *shōji*,[6] passed under the willow, and continued straight on towards the riverbed.

The old man went outside. I followed him out. A small gourd hung from his waist, and he had a square box slung over one shoulder and tucked under his arm. He wore pale yellow *momohiki* trousers[7] and a pale yellow sleeveless tunic. Only the *tabi*[8] on his feet were a brighter yellow. Something about them made me think they were made of leather.

The old man went straight to the willow. Three or four children were already there. The old man beamed jovially as he

---

5. **Obi:** A sash of thick material worn as part of a traditional Japanese outfit.

6. **Shōji:** Wooden-framed paper screens used as sliding doors and room dividers.

7. **Momohiki trousers:** Tight work trousers, associated with farmers and other laborers.

8. **Tabi:** Traditional Japanese socks dividing the big toe from the others so that *zōri* and other sandal-like footwear can be worn over them.

pulled a pale yellow *tenugui*[9] from his waist. Twisting the *tenugui* into a sort of thin rope, he placed it in the middle of the clearing and then drew a circle around it. Finally, he pulled a candy peddler's brass flute from the box slung over his shoulder.

"Any moment now, that *tenugui*'s going to turn into a snake!" he said. "Keep watching, keep watching!"

The children watched the *tenugui* intently. I watched too.

"Keep watching, keep watching!" he repeated. "Ready?" Then, playing his flute as he went, he began to circle the *tenugui* along the ring he had drawn around it. I kept my eyes fixed on the *tenugui*. It did not move a bit.

Around and around the old man went, tootling away on his flute. He walked carefully, tiptoeing in his straw *waraji*[10] sandals as if trying not to disturb the *tenugui*. The look on his face might have been fear. There also seemed to be enjoyment there.

After a time, the old man's flute fell silent. Opening the box slung over his shoulder again, he gingerly picked up the *tenugui* by its head and tossed it in.

"Now it'll turn into a snake inside the box," he said. "I'll show you any moment now — any moment now!" He began to walk straight ahead. Passing under the willow, he went straight on down a narrow path. Hoping to see the snake, I followed him down the road as far as he went. Every so often he would say, "Any moment now!" or "A snake, it'll turn into a snake!" as he walked. Finally, as we arrived at the banks of the river, he broke into song:

> *Now, any moment now, a snake it'll become,*
> *Yes, it's sure to happen now, hear the flute's song.*

---

9. **Tenugui:** A long, narrow hand towel of thin fabric.
10. **Waraji:** Sandals made of rough straw rope.

Seeing neither bridge nor boat, I thought the old man would stop here and show us the snake in his box, but he plunged forward into the river. At first the water only came up to his knees, but before long it was at his waist, and soon he had disappeared up to his chest.

Still he sang:

> *Now, getting deeper now, turning into night,*
> *Yes, going straight ahead——*

He showed no sign of stopping. His beard disappeared from view, then his face, then the top of his head, until finally even the little cap he wore was gone.

I was sure that he would show me the snake when he came out on the other side, and so I stood alone where the rushes rustled, waiting and waiting. But the old man never came back up.

The Fifth Night

The Fifth Night

*The fifth dream is a pastiche of imagery from Japan's ancient and
even mythological past. The increasing sophistication of the narrative
hints at the ways in which Sōseki will push the boundaries of the
dream conceit before the series is over.*

This is what I dreamed.

Long, long ago, perhaps almost reaching back to the Age
of the Gods[1], bad luck in battle saw me defeated, captured alive,
and dragged before the enemy chieftain.

In those days, all the men were tall. They also all let their
beards grow long. Around their waists they wore leather belts
from which they hung swords that looked like clubs. Their bows
looked like thick wisteria vines, torn straight from the tree. They
did not lacquer or even polish them before use. They were
simple and rough in the extreme.

The enemy chieftain was seated on what looked like an over-
turned sake pot. He held his bow upright, gripping it square in
the middle with his right hand and letting its lowest point rest
on the grass below. Looking at his face, I saw that his bushy
eyebrows met above his nose. In those days, of course, there was
no such thing as a razor.

---

1. **Age of the Gods:** The traditional name for the era in Japanese mythology
before the accession of the first emperor, Jimmu.

As a captive, I was not permitted a stool, so I sat cross-legged on the grass. On my feet I wore long straw boots. Such boots were deeply made back then. Mine came up to my knees when I was standing. The straw around the top had been left partly unwoven so that it hung down like a decorative fringe, rustling with each step.

The chieftain looked me in the face by the light of the bonfire and asked if I would live or die. It was customary in those days to at least ask this question of all prisoners. To choose life was to surrender, while death indicated refusal to submit. *Die*, I replied shortly. The chieftain threw aside the bow he was resting on the grass and began to draw the club-like sword that hung at his waist. The bonfire blazed in a gust of wind, sending flames flickering across the blade. I opened my right hand like a maple leaf and raised it, palm out, to just above eye level. This was a sign that meant *Wait*. The chieftain resheathed his thick sword with a metallic sound.

Even in those days they knew love. I told the chieftain that I wanted to see the woman I cared for once more before I died. The chieftain said that he would wait until dawn broke and the rooster crowed. I would have to summon the woman to me by then. If she had not arrived by the crow of the rooster, I would be killed before I could see her again.

Still seated, the chieftain gazed into the bonfire. Down on the grass with big straw boots still crossed, I waited for the woman. The night wore on.

From time to time I heard the bonfire settle. This would make the flames lick at the chieftain as if thrown off-balance. The chieftain's eyes would sparkle under his pitch-black eyebrows. Then someone would approach and throw a new armful of branches into the fire. Eventually the fire would begin to crackle. It was a valiant sound, a sound that could turn back the gloom of night.

Meanwhile, a woman was untying a white horse from the oak tree behind her house. Stroking its mane three times, she leapt lightly onto its back. She rode bareback, with no saddle or stirrups. Her long, white legs kicked the horse's flank, and it broke at once into a full gallop. Far off in the sky, she could see the faint light of the newly fed bonfire. The horse flew through the darkness towards this light. Its breath erupted from its nose like two pillars of fire as it ran. Still the woman urged it on, kicking its belly again and again with her slim legs. The horse galloped so quickly that the sky rang with the sound of its hooves. The woman's hair streamed out in the darkness behind her. But still she did not arrive at the bonfire.

Suddenly, from the side of the road where the darkness was complete, the woman heard the *Cock-a-doodle-doo!* of a rooster's crow. She leaned back, pulling sharply on the reins with both hands. The horse's two front hooves dug into the hard rock below.

Cock-a-doodle-doo! the rooster crowed again.

With a small cry of surprise, the woman let the reins go limp. The horse collapsed to its knees and pitched forward, rider and all. A deep crevice had lain just out of sight beneath the rocks.

The impression the horse's hooves left on that rock is still there today. It was the trickster Amanojaku[2] who had imitated the rooster's crow. For as long as those hoofmarks remain in the rock, Amanojaku shall be my sworn enemy.

---

2. **Amanojaku:** A malicious figure in Japanese folklore who works to thwart and subvert human desires.

The Sixth Night

The Sixth Night

Unkei was an influential Japanese Buddhist sculptor who died in 1223, but the modern narrator of the sixth dream nevertheless finds him at work at Gokoku-ji, a temple in Tokyo that was not established until 1681.

Hearing that the sculptor Unkei was carving the Two Benevolent Kings[1] at the main gate of Gokoku-ji, I decided to stroll over and take a look. I arrived to find a large crowd already gathered and vigorously exchanging opinions on the word in progress.

A large red pine stood about seven or eight yards in front of the gate, trunk stretching towards the distant blue sky at just the right angle to obscure the gate's tiled roof. The pine's green foliage and the red lacquered gate contrasted beautifully with each other. The pine was well positioned, too. Rising unobtrusively from the left of the gate, growing broader as it slanted up and across to reach the roof, it had an antiquated air, even putting me in mind of the Kamakura era.[2]

---

1. **Two Benevolent Kings:** A fearsome pair who guard the Buddha in the Mahāyāna Buddhist pantheon. Many temple gates in Japan are flanked by carvings of the Two Benevolent Kings, known as *Niō* in Japanese. The pair carved by Unkei at Tōdai-ji in Nara are particularly well known.

2. **Kamakura era:** 1185–1333 CE, the period when Unkei produced his best-known work. (He was born around 1150, in the preceding Heian era.)

But the people watching were all of the Meiji era,[3] just as I was. In fact, the larger part of the crowd was rickshaw drivers. No doubt they had grown bored of simply standing around waiting for passengers.

"Talk about big!"

"Must be a lot more work than carving a person."

As I considered this, another man spoke. "Huh, it's the Benevolent Kings. They're still carving the Benevolent Kings? You don't say! I thought that all the Benevolent Kings were old as the hills."

"They do look strong, eh?" a different man said to me. "You know what they say, right? — there's never been anyone stronger than the Two Benevolent Kings. They say they were even stronger than Yamato-Dake no Mikoto!"[4] This man had his kimono tucked up around his waist, and wore no hat. He looked decidedly uneducated.

Unkei kept his hammer and chisel in motion, utterly ignoring the commentary from his audience. He did not even glance behind him. Perched high above, he stayed hard at work carving out the faces of the Benevolent Kings.

Balanced on Unkei's head was something like a small *eboshi*[5]. I couldn't tell what his clothes were made of — perhaps rough, unlined *suō*[6] — but his loose sleeves were tied back to keep them out of the way. The effect was quite archaic. It made for a jarring contrast with his chattering audience. Why, I wondered, was Unkei still alive in the present day? It was a mystery to me, but I did not stop watching.

---

3. **Meiji era:** 1868–1912 CE. For Sōseki, the present.

4. **Yamato-Dake no Mikoto:** Another name for Yamato Takeru, a legendary prince of ancient Japan.

5. **Eboshi:** A type of hat common when Unkei was alive but archaic by Meiji times.

6. **Suō:** A simple two-piece linen garment with leather ties, also associated with the period in which Unkei lived.

Unkei, for his part, remained focused solely on his carving, apparently not finding the situation mysterious or odd in the slightest.

A young man who had been gazing up at all this turned to me. "That's Unkei for you!" he said, enrapt. "We're not even here for him. It's as if he's saying, 'The only heroes under heaven are the Benevolent Kings and I.' Just remarkable!"

Intrigued by what the man had said, I glanced towards him.

"Just look at how he uses that hammer and chisel," he continued, without even pausing. "He's transcended this world entirely — he's entered the realm of supreme freedom."

Unkei was now carving out a bushy pair of eyebrows, about an inch high. No sooner would he bring the blade of his chisel back up than his hammer would come down at an angle to strike it again. A stubby chip fell as each blow rang out, and as I watched an enraged nose emerged from the hard wood, nostrils flared. Unkei showed no hesitation as he wielded the blade. He did not appear to be troubled by even the smallest of doubts.

"Amazing that he can just throw the chisel around like that and still get the eyebrows and noses to come out the way he wants," I said, almost to myself, as if too impressed to keep my thoughts inside.

"Oh, it isn't the chisel that makes those eyebrows and noses," the young man said. "Those exact eyebrows and noses are buried in the wood, and he just uses the hammer and chisel to dig them out. It's just like digging a rock out of the ground — there's no way to get it wrong."

This was a new way to think about sculpture for me. If what the man said was true, I realized, then anyone should be able to do it. Suddenly wanting to try carving some Benevolent Kings of my own, I left the crowd to it and returned home.

I pulled a chisel and a steel hammer from my toolbox and went out into my back yard. An oak tree had fallen in a storm earlier, and I had had it chopped up into firewood, giving me a pile of pieces of wood of just the right size.

I chose the largest piece and began to carve vigorously, but unfortunately I did not find the Benevolent Kings inside. Nor, sadly, did I find them in the next piece I chose. Nor the third. One by one, I carved up every piece of firewood in the pile, but the Benevolent Kings were nowhere to be found. Finally I realized that the Benevolent Kings simply were not buried in Meiji trees. With this I more or less understood why Unkei was still alive.

The Seventh Night

The Seventh Night

The seventh dream has long been viewed as a metaphor for Japan in the Meiji era. Many at the time felt that the nation had lost its way in its attempts to modernize, yet had no way of influencing the direction in which things were moving.

I found myself aboard a great ship.

Day and night the ship cut its way through the waves, belching endless black smoke as it went. The noise was horrific. But where the ship was headed I did not know. All I saw was the sun, rising from the waves like a red-hot fire iron. It rose until it was directly over the tallest mast and then seemed to simply hang there, but before long it had passed overhead and gone ahead of the great ship. Finally, hissing like a red-hot fire iron, it would sink beneath the waves again. The boat would let out its horrific noise and give chase. But it never caught up.

Once I caught hold of a crewman. "Is this boat headed west?" I asked him.

The crewman looked at me for a moment, caution in his face. "Why?" he asked finally.

"Because we seem to be chasing the setting sun."

The crewman guffawed and walked away, leaving me where I stood. Then I heard him singing a work song:

> *The westering sun, does it end in the east?*
> *Can this be the truth?*
> *The east-risen sun, does it hail from the west?*
> *Can this too be true?*
> *Tossed on the waves, rudder for a pillow —*
> *Let it roll, let it roll!*

Heading to the bow, I saw many sailors gathered there to haul in the stout lines.

I became terribly lonely. I did not know when I would ever stand on dry land again. Nor did I know where we were headed. The only certainties were the black smoke the ship belched and the way it cut through the waves. The waves themselves stretched on and on, a seemingly limitless field of blue. Sometimes they turned purple, too. But around the ship they were always churned pure white with foam. I was terribly lonely. Better to throw myself overboard and die, I thought, than to remain on a ship like this.

Many others were on board. Most appeared to be foreigners. But there were faces of all kinds. Once, as the ship swayed under a cloudy sky, a woman clung to the handrail, weeping piteously. The handkerchief she wiped her eyes with looked white. But she wore a Western outfit, made of something like chintz. I realized when I saw her that I was not alone in my sadness.

I was gazing at the stars out on the top deck one evening when a foreigner approached and asked if I knew any astronomy. I was so bored that I wanted to die. Astronomy meant nothing to me. I ignored him. But the foreigner then began to tell me about the seven stars that crowned Taurus. The stars, he went on, the sea, all had been created by God. Finally he asked if I believed in God. I ignored him, eyes turned to the sky.

Once I entered the salon to see a splendidly dressed young woman facing away from me as she playing the piano. Beside her stood a tall, dashing man, singing alone. His mouth seemed terribly large. But the two of them appeared entirely without interest in anything outside each other. They even seemed to have forgotten that they were on a ship.

My boredom grew desperate. At last I resolved to die. So, one evening, when no-one was around, I gathered my courage and leapt overboard. Except — the moment my feet left the deck and my link with the ship was severed, I longed to live. I regretted what I had done from the bottom of my heart. But it was too late. I was headed into the sea whether I liked it or not. The ship, however, had apparently been built extraordinarily tall, and so although my body was clear of it, my feet had yet to reach the water. With nothing to catch hold of, though, I drew closer and closer to the sea. I pulled in my legs as much as I could, but still I drew closer. The water was black in color.

Meanwhile, the ship had moved on, belching the same black smoke as always. I understood for the first time that I would have been better off on board, even if I did not know where it was headed, but I could make no use of that knowledge now, and felt infinite fear and regret as I quietly fell towards the black waves.

The Eighth Night

The Eighth Night

*The eighth dream is one of the most cryptic and intricate of the series,
dwelling on sight and perspective. Notably, the narrator appears able
to see into the other dreams through the windows and mirrors of
this one, raising new questions about how
the ten dreams might be interrelated.*

Crossing the threshold of to the barber shop, I was greeted
by a chorus of *Irasshai!*[1] from several men in white who
had been waiting inside.

I stood in the middle of the square room and looked around.
Two of the walls had windows, and mirrors hung on the other
two. By my count, there were six mirrors in all.

I approached one of the mirrors and seated myself before it.
A well-stuffed cushion greeted my behind. This was a very
comfortably made chair. The mirror reflected my face splendidly. Behind my face I could see a window. I could also see
the low wooden slat screen around the raised corner of the
room where accounts were kept. There was no-one at the low
accounting desk behind the screen. The people in the street
outside were visible from the waist up as they passed the windows.

---

1. **Irasshai!:** The traditional greeting for a customer entering a place of
business.

43

Shōtarō passed by, accompanied by a woman. He was wearing a Panama hat that he must have bought since I saw him last — and the woman, too; when had he made her acquaintance? It was quite beyond me. He seemed most pleased with both of his new finds. As I tried to get a proper look at the woman's face, they passed out of sight.

A tofu peddler blowing a trumpet went past. His cheeks swelled as if stung by bees as he held the trumpet to his mouth. They were still swollen as he passed out of sight, which weighed heavily on my mind. It made me feel as if he would stay beestung for the rest of his life.

A geisha appeared. Her face was not yet powdered white. Her Shimada hairstyle[2] sagged at the base, and looked sloppily done overall. Her face still looked half-asleep. Her color was so poor that I almost felt sorry for her. She bowed and greeted someone, but whoever it was did not appear in the mirror.

Just then a large man in white approached me from behind, scissors and comb in hand, and began examining my hair. Twisting my thin whiskers, I asked him what he thought — could he do anything with it? Without saying a word, the man in white tapped me lightly on the head with the amber comb he held in his hand.

"Yes, my hair, too; what do you think? Can you do anything with it?" I asked the man in white. He did not reply, but began snipping away with his scissors.

I watched closely in the mirror, keeping my eyes wide open so as not to miss anything, but with each snip of the scissors a lock of black hair flew towards me, and eventually I lost my nerve and closed my eyes again. Upon which the man in white spoke.

"Did Sir see the goldfish peddler outside?"

---

2. **Shimada hairstyle:** A traditional Japanese hairstyle, with the hair arranged up in a type of bun—usually worn by young women.

I did not, I replied. The man in white snipped on, saying nothing more. Just then, someone suddenly cried, ——Look out! My eyes flew open and I saw the wheel of a bicycle framed by the man in white's arm. I saw a rickshaw's pole. But then the man in white placed both hands on my head and turned it firmly to the side. I could no longer see the bicycle or the rickshaw at all. The scissors snipped away.

Eventually, the man in white stepped around to my side and began trimming around my ears. Now that locks of hair had stopped flying around, I could open my eyes without fear. ——Awamochi[3] here, mochi, mochi, someone called from quite near. They were keeping time by pounding the mochi in a small mortar and pestle as they chanted. I had not seen an awamochi peddler since I was a child, and I wished I could see this one. But they never appeared in the mirror. The sound of mochi being pounded was the closest I got.

I peered into the corner of the mirror, straining my vision to the limit. Suddenly, I realized that there was now a woman kneeling behind the slat screen. She was dark of complexion, with thick eyebrows and a heavy build, had her hair up in an Ichō-gaeshi hairstyle,[4] and wore a plain suawase over a black juban.[5] She was counting a stack of bills. They looked like ten-yen bills to me. She lowered her long eyelashes and pursed her thin lips, focusing intently and counting at a remarkable speed. Nevertheless, there seemed to be no end to the bills. There couldn't have been more than a hundred or so in her lap, but those hundred bills remained a hundred bills no matter how long she counted.

---

3. **Awamochi:** Pounded cakes (mochi) made of foxtail millet (awa).

4. **Ichō-gaeshi hairstyle:** Another traditional Japanese hairstyle, associated with women in service positions and a slightly older age range than the Shimada.

5. **Plain suawase over a black juban:** A simple, unlined kimono worn over a black inner garment—a far from glamorous look.

I stared absently at the woman's face and the ten-yen bills. Then, in a loud voice right by my ear, the man in white said, "Let's get you shampooed." It was just the chance I needed, so as soon as I rose from the chair I looked back over towards the counter. But behind the counter I could see neither the woman nor the bills nor anything else.

Paying my bill and leaving the barber shop, I saw five small oval tubs lined up in the street to the left of the doorway. The tubs were full of goldfish: red goldfish, spotted goldfish, skinny goldfish, fat goldfish, and many other kinds. The goldfish peddler sat behind them. Chin in hand, he sat gazing at the goldfish lined up before him, completely motionless. The bustle and movement all around did not seem to bother him at all. I stood there for a while watching him, but I did not see him move once the entire time.

The Ninth Night

The Ninth Night

As with the second dream, many scholars see echoes of Sōseki's own childhood in this story. That the violent internal struggles of Japan's Meiji Restoration began one year after Sōseki himself was born is suggestive.

There were rumblings of unrest abroad. War seemed ready to break out at any time. Unsaddled horses fleeing burned-out stables seemed to gallop around the house day and night, chased by unruly guardsmen. Within the house, however, all was quiet and still.

In the house were a young mother and her child, almost in his third year. The child's father had left for parts unknown. He had set out on a night with no moon. He had pulled his straw *waraji*[1] onto his feet, donned a black hood, and gone out the side door. The mother had been holding a *bonbori* lantern[2] from which the light fell long and thin into the dark night, illuminating the old cypress by the hedge.

The child's father never came back. Every day, the mother would ask her child, "Where's Daddy?" The child did not say anything. Eventually he began to reply, "Away." When the mother asked, "When will he be home?" the child would smile

---

1. **Waraji:** Sandals made of rough straw rope.
2. **Bonbori lantern:** A paper lantern with a square wooden frame.

and say "Away" again. This would make the mother smile too. Then she would repeat to the child, over and over, "He will be home soon." The child, though, only learned to say "Soon." Sometimes he would reply "Soon" when she asked him "Where's Daddy?" too.

Once night had fallen and it had grown quiet outside, the mother would retie her *obi*[3] around her waist, slipping into it a short sword in a sharkskin scabbard, tie the child to her back with another, narrower *obi*, and then duck out through the side gate. She always wore *zōri*[4] on her feet. The sound of these *zōri* was sometimes enough to lull the child to sleep.

The mother would walk west, leaving the earthen walls of the houses behind, until she reached the bottom of the hill where the great ginkgo tree stood. Cutting right at the ginkgo tree, she would continue another hundred yards or so until she saw the *torii*[5] off to the right, at the end of a path with a rice paddy on one side and nothing but bamboo scrub on the other. Beyond the *torii* was a dark stand of cedar trees. After that, she would walk another forty stone-paved yards before arriving at the foot of the stairs leading up to the old shrine. Above the offering box, which had been washed a dull gray, a rope hung from a large bell, and in the daytime a framed sign could be seen hanging beside the bell which read "Hachiman-gū."[6] The first character on the sign was drawn in an interesting way, like two pigeons facing each other. Many other framed offerings hung there too. Most were gold-papered *kinteki*[7] accompanied by the names of the warriors that had shot an arrow through them. Here and there a sword had been offered up as well.

---

3. **Obi:** A sash of thick material worn as part of a traditional Japanese outfit.

4. **Zōri:** Flat traditional sandals, more refined than *waraji*.

5. **Torii:** The distinctive gateway found outside shrines.

6. **Hachiman-gū:** A shrine dedicated to Hachiman, tutelary god of warriors.

7. **Kinteki:** A small archery target with gold paper stretched over it used in traditional Japanese archery.

Past the *torii*, there were always owls hooting in the branches of the cedars. The mother's rough *zōri* slapped wetly on the ground. Once they reached the temple and the sound stopped, the mother would first ring the bell, then immediately drop to a crouch and bring her hands together. The owls usually fell silent at this point. The mother would then pray fiercely for the safety of her husband. Her husband, she reasoned, was a samurai, while Hachiman was god of the bow; surely prayers as fervent as hers would not go entirely unheard.

The child would often wake at the sound of the bell and, scared by the surrounding darkness, burst into tears on the mother's back. At such times, the mother would not stop mumbling her prayers, but she would jog the child gently on her back soothingly. Sometimes this was enough to stop the child crying. Sometimes it just made things worse. Either way, the mother did not rise from her crouch lightly.

Once she had made all the prayers for her husband's safety that she could, the mother would loosen the narrow *obi* around her back and bring the child around to her front, holding him in her arms as she climbed the stairs to the shrine proper. "Be good, now," she would say, rubbing her cheek close against his. "I won't be long." Then she would slip the narrow *obi* off entirely, tie one end around the child, and loop the other through the railing on the shrine's porch. This done, she would descend the staircase again to begin the task of treading back and forth across the forty yards of paved stone one hundred times to seal her petition.

Left tied to the temple, the child would crawl about its broad porch in the darkness as far as the *obi* would allow. Nights like this were a great relief to the mother. When the tied-up child cried and wept, on the other hand, she would be driven to distraction. The pace of her hundred repetitions across the courtyard would pick up dramatically. She would become terribly out of breath. Sometimes she had no option but to interrupt her pacing to climb the stairs to the shrine proper, soothe the child any way she could, and then begin her hundred repetitions again.

The mother spent countless fretful nights this way, unable to sleep for worry over the child's father — but he was long since dead, slain by a masterless samurai.

This sad tale I heard from my mother in a dream.

The Tenth Night

The Tenth Night

*The series finishes with the uneasy comedy of the tenth story —
which, read carefully, contains no indication that it is a dream at all.*

Shōtarō had come home in the evening, seven days after the
woman took him away, and immediately gone to bed with a
fever — or so I heard from Ken, who had visited to give me the
news.

Shōtarō was the best-looking man in the neighborhood, and
impeccably honest and upright to boot. He had just one vice.
When evening fell, he would put on his Panama hat, seat himself outside the fruit shop, and gaze at the faces of the women
passing by. He always found much to admire in them. Outside
of this hobby, he had no particular quirks worth mentioning.

When women were scarce, he would give up on the foot
traffic and look at the fruit instead. All kinds of fruit were
there: peaches, apples, loquats, bananas, all neatly arranged in
two rows of baskets, ready for use as visiting gifts.
——Beautiful, Shōtarō would murmur, gazing at the baskets.
If I were to go into business, it'd have to be a fruit shop. Not,
of course, that he ever did anything but loaf around in his
Panama hat.

——Such a pretty color, he might say, admiring, for example, some *natsumikan*.[1] But he had never actually put down the money to buy any of the fruit, and of course none of the fruit could be eaten for free. Praising their color was as far as he went.

One evening, a woman had suddenly appeared outside the store. She had appeared to be of some standing in society, and had been splendidly dressed. Shōtarō had been utterly entranced by the colors of her kimono. He had also found much to admire in her face. Doffing his Panama hat, he had greeted her cordially; she had responded by pointing at the largest basket of fruit and saying, ——That one, please. Shōtarō had handed it to her at once. The woman had held it in one hand for a moment before saying, ——My, how heavy it is!

Unburdened by other obligations and solicitous by nature, Shōtarō had volunteered to help the woman carry her fruit home, and left the store with her. He had never come back.

Shōtarō had always been irresponsible, but this was too much even for him. After seven days his family and friends had begun to fear the worst, and just as they were raising the alarm he had casually strolled home again. Everyone crowded around to ask where he had gone, and he told them a story of riding a train into the mountains.

It must have been a remarkably long train ride. As Shōtarō told the story, when the train stopped he had disembarked to find himself in a meadow, so large that he had seen nothing but green grass in every direction. He had walked across the grass with the woman until suddenly they were at the edge of a cliff.

——Now, the woman had said to him, jump. Peering over the edge, Shōtarō had seen the face of the cliff, but could not see the ground below. Doffing his Panama hat again, he had made several polite demurrals. ——If you don't jump, the woman had

---

1. **Natsumikan:** An orange-yellow citrus fruit about the size of a grapefruit.

said, you will be licked by a pig; are you quite sure? There were two things Shōtarō despised: pigs, and the *rōkyoku* singer Kumoemon.[2] He did not, however, despise either of them more than he valued his life, and so he had again refused to jump. At that moment, a pig had appeared, snuffling as it came. Seeing no other option, Shōtarō had struck the pig across the snout with his betelwood walking stick. The pig rolled over the edge of the cliff with an oink. Shōtarō had barely breathed a sigh of relief before another pig had begun nuzzling him with its large snout. Once more he had no option but to raise his walking stick. Once more the pig had oinked and tumbled upside-down into the pit. And then yet another pig appeared. This was when Shōtarō had happened to glance up and realize that a whole herd of pigs, a line of countless thousands stretching out to the edge of the grassy meadow, were noisily making their way directly to where he stood at the edge of the cliff. Terror had gripped his heart. Still, with no other options, all he could do was strike the pigs across the snout with his walking stick one by one as they arrived. Mysteriously, the pigs would roll over the edge of the cliff as soon as the stick touched their snouts. Peering over the precipice, Shōtarō had seen a whole column of upside-down pigs falling down the cliff face into the apparently bottomless depths. The idea that he had sent so many pigs over the cliff had scared even him. But the pigs had been relentless. They had been like a dark cloud with legs, oinking and inexhaustible as they trampled the fresh green grass.

Shōtarō had put up a heroic fight, beating pigs across the snout for six nights and seven days. Eventually, however, his energy dwindled, his hands became weak as *konnyaku*,[3] and

---

2. **The *rōkyoku* singer Kumoemon:** *Rōkyoku* was a popular music genre during the Meiji period. Kumoemon was one of the best known and most popular exponents of the form.

3. **Konnyaku:** A rubbery yam cake made from the root of the konjac plant.

finally he had been licked by a pig. With that, he had collapsed at the edge of the cliff.

——So you see, too much girl-watching can be bad for you, Ken said as he concluded his story. I had to agree. But Ken had also been talking about how he wanted Shōtarō's Panama hat.

Shōtarō was doomed. That Panama was as good as Ken's.

The Cat's Grave

The Cat's Grave

First published in 1909, this autobiographical vignette details an episode from the previous year, just after the Ten Nights Dreaming *stories were published. The cat in the story was the model for the title character in the satirical* I Am A Cat *(1905), Sōseki's first major success as a novelist.*

A fter our move to Waseda, the cat began to grow thinner and thinner. He no longer showed any interest in playing with the children. Whenever the sun was out, all he would do was lie on the *engawa*,[1] not moving a muscle, square chin on his neatly arranged paws as he stared out at the bushes in the garden. No matter how rowdily the children played nearby, he did not deign to notice them. The children, for their part, had long since given up on the cat. Obviously finding him no fun any more, they treated this old friend of theirs like a stranger. Nor were they the only ones: the maid put out food for the cat three times a day in the corner of the kitchen, but had little time for him otherwise. Worse yet, most of what she put out was gobbled up by a big calico who lived nearby and visited just for this purpose. Our cat did not seem particularly angered by this. I never saw fight. He just lay there. There was, however, a certain joylessness in

---

1. **Engawa:** A wooden veranda running around the edge of a traditional Japanese house.

his repose. He did not look like someone stretching out to luxu-
riate in the sun's rays; rather, he seemed to lack any *way* to
move — no, this does not fully describe it. It appeared that his
listlessness had grown so great that, as lonely as it was to stay
unmoving, to move would have been still lonelier, leaving him
with no choice but to stay where he was, enduring things as best
he could. His gaze was always fixed on the garden, but I doubt
he saw the leaves on the bushes, or the shapes in which they
grew. That was just where his greenish-yellow eyes happened to
be resting. Just as the children no longer recognized his existence, he did not seem to clearly register the existence of the
world around him either.

Still, he did go out from time to time, apparently with business to attend to. Every time he did so, however, the calico cat
that lived nearby would give chase. Terrified, our cat would leap
back up onto our veranda and burst through the paper of the
closed *shōji*[2] screens to take refuge by the hearth inside. Those
were the only times that we noticed his existence. No doubt they
were also the only times that he was fully aware that he was
alive.

As these things went on, the fur began to fall out of the cat's
long tail. At first it just seemed dimpled here and there, but then
patches of raw skin began to spread, and the whole thing
drooped in a way that was pitiful to see. He took to twisting and
straining his body, already weary enough with everything, to lick
at his sore spots.

—Hey, I grunted to my wife. Looks like something's wrong
with the cat. —Yes, I think he's just getting old, she replied,
supremely indifferent. I let the matter pass as well. Not long
afterwards, though, the cat began to bring up his food from time
to time. His throat would pulse violently as he let out a painful-

---

2. **Shōji:** Translucent paper screens stretched over a light wooden framework
and used in place of walls and partitions in Japanese architecture.

sounding noise somewhere between a sneeze and a hiccup. Painful as it sounded, though, I had no choice but to chase him outside whenever I noticed him like this. Otherwise, he would have soiled the *tatami*[3] or the *futon*[4] without a second thought. Most of the large *zabuton*[5] we had set aside for visitors were ruined this way.

"We have to do something. It's probably a stomach bug — stir some Hōtan[6] in with his drinking water."

My wife didn't say anything. Two or three days later, I asked if she had given the cat any Hōtan to drink. —It's no use trying to make him drink, she replied. He won't open his mouth. He throws up whenever he eats fishbones, she added by way of explanation. —Well, why don't you stop giving them to him, then? I replied, rather roughly, before returning to my reading.

Nausea gone, the cat went back to quietly lying around as he had before. By now he was curling himself up tightly, huddled and still, as if he had nothing left to rely on but the *engawa* that held him up. The look in his eyes also began to change. In the beginning there had been a certain steadiness in the melancholy of his gaze, as if he were staring at something too far away to focus on. But this was giving way to an uncertain, incessant motion. Meanwhile, the color in his eyes was sinking deeper and deeper. It put me in mind of flickering lightning as the sun went down. But I let this pass too. Nor did my wife appear to pay it any mind. The children, of course, had forgotten that they ever had a cat.

One evening, the cat had been stretched out on its stomach at the edge of the children's bedding for a while when he suddenly let out a throaty groan, as if he had caught a fish only to

---

3. **Tatami:** Woven, stuffed mats used for flooring.
4. **Futon:** A quilted mattress used for sleeping.
5. **Zabuton:** A smaller cushion used for sitting.
6. **Hōtan:** A patent medicine for stomach ailments.

suddenly have it snatched away. I thought it strange at the time, but no-one else noticed it. The children were sound asleep. My wife was engrossed in her sewing. A short time later, the cat groaned again. My wife's hands finally paused. —What's wrong with him? I asked. We don't want him biting the children on the head or something during the night. —Oh, he would never, my wife said, and went back to sewing the sleeve of her *juban*.[7] The cat kept up his occasional groaning.

He then spent the entire following day groaning as he lay at the hearth. Tasks like making the tea and bringing in the kettle, I understand, were rather unsettling that day. But once night fell my wife and I both forgot about the cat entirely. In fact, that very evening was when the cat died. The maid found his body when she went to get some firewood from the shed in the yard the following morning, already stiff and lying on top of an old stove.

My wife made a point of going out to see the cat's body for herself. From that point on, her previous indifference was replaced by industrious concern. She sent one of our regular rickshaw boys out to buy a square grave marker, which she asked me to write something on. I wrote "HERE LIES THE CAT" on the front, and composed a short poem for the back: *Comes the lightning/ Here beneath/ As evening falls.* —Can I bury it as it is? asked the rickshaw boy. —What else are we going to do, have it cremated? said the maid witheringly.

The children, too, suddenly found a new fondness for the cat. They adorned his grave marker with glass bottles on either side, stuffed with bush clover. They also filled a small rice bowl with water to place before the grave. Both flowers and water were both changed daily. On the evening of the third day, I watched from the window of my study as one of our girls, almost in her

---

7. **Juban:** An undergarment worn under kimono.

fourth year[8], approached the grave alone. After staring at the plain wooden marker for a while, she dipped a toy ladle she was carrying into the water that had been offered to the cat, scooping some up to drink. Nor was this the only time she did this. That little splash of water strewn with clover blossom petals quenched Aiko's thirst any number of times in the quiet of the evening.

Each month, on the anniversary of the cat's death, my wife makes sure to place a bowl of rice topped with dried bonito and salmon before his grave. She has yet to forget a single month. Lately, though, rather than taking the offering out to the garden, she seems content with leaving it on top of the chest of drawers in the living room.

---

8. **Almost in her fourth year:** By the traditional Japanese system of reckoning ages; as calculated by the Western system, she was just over two-and-a-half years old at the time of this story.

DOVER·THRIFT·EDITIONS

POETRY

101 GREAT AMERICAN POEMS, Edited by The American Poetry & Literacy Project. (0-486-40158-8)

100 BEST-LOVED POEMS, Edited by Philip Smith. (0-486-28553-7)

ENGLISH ROMANTIC POETRY: An Anthology, Edited by Stanley Appelbaum. (0-486-29282-7)

THE INFERNO, Dante Alighieri. Translated and with notes by Henry Wadsworth Longfellow. (0-486-44288-8)

PARADISE LOST, John Milton. Introduction and Notes by John A. Himes. (0-486-44287-X)

SPOON RIVER ANTHOLOGY, Edgar Lee Masters. (0-486-27275-3)

SELECTED CANTERBURY TALES, Geoffrey Chaucer. (0-486-28241-4)

SELECTED POEMS, Emily Dickinson. (0-486-26466-1)

LEAVES OF GRASS: The Original 1855 Edition, Walt Whitman. (0-486-45676-5)

COMPLETE SONNETS, William Shakespeare. (0-486-26686-9)

THE RAVEN AND OTHER FAVORITE POEMS, Edgar Allan Poe. (0-486-26685-0)

ENGLISH VICTORIAN POETRY: An Anthology, Edited by Paul Negri. (0-486-40425-0)

SELECTED POEMS, Walt Whitman. (0-486-26878-0)

THE ROAD NOT TAKEN AND OTHER POEMS, Robert Frost. (0-486-27550-7)

AFRICAN-AMERICAN POETRY: An Anthology, 1773-1927, Edited by Joan R. Sherman. (0-486-29604-0)

GREAT SHORT POEMS, Edited by Paul Negri. (0-486-41105-2)

THE RIME OF THE ANCIENT MARINER, Samuel Taylor Coleridge. (0-486-27266-4)

THE WASTE LAND, PRUFROCK AND OTHER POEMS, T. S. Eliot. (0-486-40061-1)

SONG OF MYSELF, Walt Whitman. (0-486-41410-8)

AENEID, Vergil. (0-486-28749-1)

SONGS FOR THE OPEN ROAD: Poems of Travel and Adventure, Edited by The American Poetry & Literacy Project. (0-486-40646-6)

SONGS OF INNOCENCE AND SONGS OF EXPERIENCE, William Blake. (0-486-27051-3)

WORLD WAR ONE BRITISH POETS: Brooke, Owen, Sassoon, Rosenberg and Others, Edited by Candace Ward. (0-486-29568-0)

GREAT SONNETS, Edited by Paul Negri. (0-486-28052-7)

CHRISTMAS CAROLS: Complete Verses, Edited by Shane Weller. (0-486-27397-0)

DOVER · THRIFT · EDITIONS

POETRY

GREAT POEMS BY AMERICAN WOMEN: An Anthology, Edited by Susan L. Rattiner. (0-486-40164-2)

FAVORITE POEMS, Henry Wadsworth Longfellow. (0-486-27273-7)

BHAGAVADGITA, Translated by Sir Edwin Arnold. (0-486-27782-8)

ESSAY ON MAN AND OTHER POEMS, Alexander Pope. (0-486-28053-5)

GREAT LOVE POEMS, Edited by Shane Weller. (0-486-27284-2)

DOVER BEACH AND OTHER POEMS, Matthew Arnold. (0-486-28037-3)

THE SHOOTING OF DAN MCGREW AND OTHER POEMS, Robert Service. (0-486-27556-6)

THE BALLAD OF READING GAOL AND OTHER POEMS, Oscar Wilde. (0-486-27072-6)

SELECTED POEMS OF RUMI, Jalalu'l-Din Rumi. (0-486-41583-X)

SELECTED POEMS OF GERARD MANLEY HOPKINS, Gerard Manley Hopkins. Edited and with an Introduction by Bob Blaisdell. (0-486-47867-X)

RENASCENCE AND OTHER POEMS, Edna St. Vincent Millay. (0-486-26873-X)

THE RUBÁIYÁT OF OMAR KHAYYÁM: First and Fifth Editions, Edward FitzGerald. (0-486-26467-X)

TO MY HUSBAND AND OTHER POEMS, Anne Bradstreet. (0-486-41408-6)

LITTLE ORPHANT ANNIE AND OTHER POEMS, James Whitcomb Riley. (0-486-28260-0)

IMAGIST POETRY: AN ANTHOLOGY, Edited by Bob Blaisdell. (0-486-40875-2)

FIRST FIG AND OTHER POEMS, Edna St. Vincent Millay. (0-486-41104-4)

GREAT SHORT POEMS FROM ANTIQUITY TO THE TWENTIETH CENTURY, Edited by Dorothy Belle Pollack. (0-486-47876-9)

THE FLOWERS OF EVIL & PARIS SPLEEN: Selected Poems, Charles Baudelaire. Translated by Wallace Fowlie. (0-486-47545-X)

CIVIL WAR SHORT STORIES AND POEMS, Edited by Bob Blaisdell. (0-486-48226-X)

EARLY POEMS, Edna St. Vincent Millay. (0-486-43672-1)

JABBERWOCKY AND OTHER POEMS, Lewis Carroll. (0-486-41582-1)

THE METAMORPHOSES: Selected Stories in Verse, Ovid. (0-486-42758-7)

IDYLLS OF THE KING, Alfred, Lord Tennyson. Edited by W. J. Rolfe. (0-486-43795-7)

A BOY'S WILL AND NORTH OF BOSTON, Robert Frost. (0-486-26866-7)

100 FAVORITE ENGLISH AND IRISH POEMS, Edited by Clarence C. Strowbridge. (0-486-44429-5)

DOVER · THRIFT · EDITIONS

FICTION

FLATLAND: A ROMANCE OF MANY DIMENSIONS, Edwin A. Abbott.
(0-486-27263-X)

PRIDE AND PREJUDICE, Jane Austen. (0-486-28473-5)

CIVIL WAR SHORT STORIES AND POEMS, Edited by Bob Blaisdell.
(0-486-48226-X)

THE DECAMERON: Selected Tales, Giovanni Boccaccio. Edited by Bob Blaisdell. (0-486-41113-3)

JANE EYRE, Charlotte Brontë. (0-486-42449-9)

WUTHERING HEIGHTS, Emily Brontë. (0-486-29256-8)

THE THIRTY-NINE STEPS, John Buchan. (0-486-28201-5)

ALICE'S ADVENTURES IN WONDERLAND, Lewis Carroll. (0-486-27543-4)

MY ÁNTONIA, Willa Cather. (0-486-28240-6)

THE AWAKENING, Kate Chopin. (0-486-27786-0)

HEART OF DARKNESS, Joseph Conrad. (0-486-26464-5)

LORD JIM, Joseph Conrad. (0-486-40650-4)

THE RED BADGE OF COURAGE, Stephen Crane. (0-486-26465-3)

THE WORLD'S GREATEST SHORT STORIES, Edited by James Daley.
(0-486-44716-2)

A CHRISTMAS CAROL, Charles Dickens. (0-486-26865-9)

GREAT EXPECTATIONS, Charles Dickens. (0-486-41586-4)

A TALE OF TWO CITIES, Charles Dickens. (0-486-40651-2)

CRIME AND PUNISHMENT, Fyodor Dostoyevsky. Translated by Constance Garnett. (0-486-41587-2)

THE ADVENTURES OF SHERLOCK HOLMES, Sir Arthur Conan Doyle.
(0-486-47491-7)

THE HOUND OF THE BASKERVILLES, Sir Arthur Conan Doyle. (0-486-28214-7)

BLAKE: PROPHET AGAINST EMPIRE, David V. Erdman. (0-486-26719-9)

WHERE ANGELS FEAR TO TREAD, E. M. Forster. (0-486-27791-7)

BEOWULF, Translated by R. K. Gordon. (0-486-27264-8)

THE RETURN OF THE NATIVE, Thomas Hardy. (0-486-43165-7)

THE SCARLET LETTER, Nathaniel Hawthorne. (0-486-28048-9)

SIDDHARTHA, Hermann Hesse. (0-486-40653-9)

THE ODYSSEY, Homer. (0-486-40654-7)

THE TURN OF THE SCREW, Henry James. (0-486-26684-2)

DUBLINERS, James Joyce. (0-486-26870-5)

DOVER · THRIFT · EDITIONS

FICTION

THE METAMORPHOSIS AND OTHER STORIES, Franz Kafka. (0-486-29030-1)

SONS AND LOVERS, D. H. Lawrence. (0-486-42121-X)

THE CALL OF THE WILD, Jack London. (0-486-26472-6)

SHAKESPEARE ILLUSTRATED: Art by Arthur Rackham, Edmund Dulac, Charles Robinson and Others, Selected and Edited by Jeff A. Menges. (0-486-47890-4)

GREAT AMERICAN SHORT STORIES, Edited by Paul Negri. (0-486-42119-8)

THE GOLD-BUG AND OTHER TALES, Edgar Allan Poe. (0-486-26875-6)

ANTHEM, Ayn Rand. (0-486-49277-X)

FRANKENSTEIN, Mary Shelley. (0-486-28211-2)

THE JUNGLE, Upton Sinclair. (0-486-41923-1)

THREE LIVES, Gertrude Stein. (0-486-28059-4)

THE STRANGE CASE OF DR. JEKYLL AND MR. HYDE, Robert Louis Stevenson. (0-486-26688-5)

DRACULA, Bram Stoker. (0-486-41109-5)

UNCLE TOM'S CABIN, Harriet Beecher Stowe. (0-486-44028-1)

ADVENTURES OF HUCKLEBERRY FINN, Mark Twain. (0-486-28061-6)

THE ADVENTURES OF TOM SAWYER, Mark Twain. (0-486-40077-8)

CANDIDE, Voltaire. Edited by Francois-Marie Arouet. (0-486-26689-3)

THE COUNTRY OF THE BLIND: and Other Science-Fiction Stories, H. G. Wells. Edited by Martin Gardner. (0-486-48289-8)

THE WAR OF THE WORLDS, H. G. Wells. (0-486-29506-0)

ETHAN FROME, Edith Wharton. (0-486-26690-7)

THE PICTURE OF DORIAN GRAY, Oscar Wilde. (0-486-27807-7)

MONDAY OR TUESDAY: Eight Stories, Virginia Woolf. (0-486-29453-6)

DOVER · THRIFT · EDITIONS

NONFICTION

POETICS, Aristotle. (0-486-29577-X)

MEDITATIONS, Marcus Aurelius. (0-486-29823-X)

THE WAY OF PERFECTION, St. Teresa of Avila. Edited and Translated by
E. Allison Peers. (0-486-48451-3)

THE DEVIL'S DICTIONARY, Ambrose Bierce. (0-486-27542-6)

GREAT SPEECHES OF THE 20TH CENTURY, Edited by Bob Blaisdell.
(0-486-47467-4)

THE COMMUNIST MANIFESTO AND OTHER REVOLUTIONARY WRITINGS:
Marx, Marat, Paine, Mao Tse-Tung, Gandhi and Others, Edited by Bob Blaisdell.
(0-486-42465-0)

INFAMOUS SPEECHES: From Robespierre to Osama bin Laden, Edited by Bob
Blaisdell. (0-486-47849-1)

GREAT ENGLISH ESSAYS: From Bacon to Chesterton, Edited by Bob Blaisdell.
(0-486-44082-6)

GREEK AND ROMAN ORATORY, Edited by Bob Blaisdell. (0-486-49622-8)

THE UNITED STATES CONSTITUTION: The Full Text with Supplementary
Materials, Edited and with supplementary materials by Bob Blaisdell.
(0-486-47166-7)

GREAT SPEECHES BY NATIVE AMERICANS, Edited by Bob Blaisdell.
(0-486-41122-2)

GREAT SPEECHES BY AFRICAN AMERICANS: Frederick Douglass, Sojourner
Truth, Dr. Martin Luther King, Jr., Barack Obama, and Others, Edited by
James Daley. (0-486-44761-8)

GREAT SPEECHES BY AMERICAN WOMEN, Edited by James Daley.
(0-486-46141-6)

HISTORY'S GREATEST SPEECHES, Edited by James Daley. (0-486-49739-9)

GREAT INAUGURAL ADDRESSES, Edited by James Daley. (0-486-44577-1)

GREAT SPEECHES ON GAY RIGHTS, Edited by James Daley. (0-486-47512-3)

ON THE ORIGIN OF SPECIES: By Means of Natural Selection, Charles Darwin.
(0-486-45006-6)

NARRATIVE OF THE LIFE OF FREDERICK DOUGLASS, Frederick Douglass.
(0-486-28499-9)

THE SOULS OF BLACK FOLK, W. E. B. Du Bois. (0-486-28041-1)

NATURE AND OTHER ESSAYS, Ralph Waldo Emerson. (0-486-46947-6)

SELF-RELIANCE AND OTHER ESSAYS, Ralph Waldo Emerson. (0-486-27790-9)

THE LIFE OF OLAUDAH EQUIANO, Olaudah Equiano. (0-486-40661-X)

WIT AND WISDOM FROM POOR RICHARD'S ALMANACK, Benjamin Franklin.
(0-486-40891-4)

THE AUTOBIOGRAPHY OF BENJAMIN FRANKLIN, Benjamin Franklin.
(0-486-29073-5)

DOVER·THRIFT·EDITIONS

NONFICTION

THE DECLARATION OF INDEPENDENCE AND OTHER GREAT DOCUMENTS OF AMERICAN HISTORY: 1775-1865, Edited by John Grafton. (0-486-41124-9)

INCIDENTS IN THE LIFE OF A SLAVE GIRL, Harriet Jacobs. (0-486-41931-2)

GREAT SPEECHES, Abraham Lincoln. (0-486-26872-1)

THE WIT AND WISDOM OF ABRAHAM LINCOLN: A Book of Quotations, Abraham Lincoln. Edited by Bob Blaisdell. (0-486-44097-4)

THE SECOND TREATISE OF GOVERNMENT AND A LETTER CONCERNING TOLERATION, John Locke. (0-486-42464-2)

THE PRINCE, Niccolò Machiavelli. (0-486-27274-5)

MICHEL DE MONTAIGNE: Selected Essays, Michel de Montaigne. Translated by Charles Cotton. Edited by William Carew Hazlitt. (0-486-48603-6)

UTOPIA, Sir Thomas More. (0-486-29583-4)

BEYOND GOOD AND EVIL: Prelude to a Philosophy of the Future, Friedrich Nietzsche. (0-486-29868-X)

TWELVE YEARS A SLAVE, Solomon Northup. (0-486-78962-4)

COMMON SENSE, Thomas Paine. (0-486-29602-4)

BOOK OF AFRICAN-AMERICAN QUOTATIONS, Edited by Joslyn Pine. (0-486-47589-1)

THE TRIAL AND DEATH OF SOCRATES: Four Dialogues, Plato. (0-486-27066-1)

THE REPUBLIC, Plato. (0-486-41121-4)

SIX GREAT DIALOGUES: Apology, Crito, Phaedo, Phaedrus, Symposium, The Republic, Plato. Translated by Benjamin Jowett. (0-486-45465-7)

WOMEN'S WIT AND WISDOM: A Book of Quotations, Edited by Susan L. Rattiner. (0-486-41123-0)

GREAT SPEECHES, Franklin Delano Roosevelt. (0-486-40894-9)

THE CONFESSIONS OF ST. AUGUSTINE, St. Augustine. (0-486-42466-9)

A MODEST PROPOSAL AND OTHER SATIRICAL WORKS, Jonathan Swift. (0-486-28759-9)

THE IMITATION OF CHRIST, Thomas à Kempis. Translated by Aloysius Croft and Harold Bolton. (0-486-43185-1)

CIVIL DISOBEDIENCE AND OTHER ESSAYS, Henry David Thoreau. (0-486-27563-9)

WALDEN; OR, LIFE IN THE WOODS, Henry David Thoreau. (0-486-28495-6)

NARRATIVE OF SOJOURNER TRUTH, Sojourner Truth. (0-486-29899-X)

THE WIT AND WISDOM OF MARK TWAIN: A Book of Quotations, Mark Twain. (0-486-40664-4)

UP FROM SLAVERY, Booker T. Washington. (0-486-28738-6)

A VINDICATION OF THE RIGHTS OF WOMAN, Mary Wollstonecraft. (0-486-29036-0)

DOVER·THRIFT·EDITIONS

PLAYS

THE ORESTEIA TRILOGY: Agamemnon, the Libation-Bearers and the Furies, Aeschylus. (0-486-29242-8)

EVERYMAN, Anonymous. (0-486-28726-2)

THE BIRDS, Aristophanes. (0-486-40886-8)

LYSISTRATA, Aristophanes. (0-486-28225-2)

THE CHERRY ORCHARD, Anton Chekhov. (0-486-26682-6)

THE SEA GULL, Anton Chekhov. (0-486-40656-3)

MEDEA, Euripides. (0-486-27548-5)

FAUST, PART ONE, Johann Wolfgang von Goethe. (0-486-28046-2)

THE INSPECTOR GENERAL, Nikolai Gogol. (0-486-28500-6)

SHE STOOPS TO CONQUER, Oliver Goldsmith. (0-486-26867-5)

GHOSTS, Henrik Ibsen. (0-486-29852-3)

A DOLL'S HOUSE, Henrik Ibsen. (0-486-27062-9)

HEDDA GABLER, Henrik Ibsen. (0-486-26469-6)

DR. FAUSTUS, Christopher Marlowe. (0-486-28208-2)

TARTUFFE, Molière. (0-486-41117-6)

BEYOND THE HORIZON, Eugene O'Neill. (0-486-29085-9)

THE EMPEROR JONES, Eugene O'Neill. (0-486-29268-1)

CYRANO DE BERGERAC, Edmond Rostand. (0-486-41119-2)

MEASURE FOR MEASURE: Unabridged, William Shakespeare. (0-486-40889-2)

FOUR GREAT TRAGEDIES: Hamlet, Macbeth, Othello, and Romeo and Juliet, William Shakespeare. (0-486-44083-4)

THE COMEDY OF ERRORS, William Shakespeare. (0-486-42461-8)

HENRY V, William Shakespeare. (0-486-42887-7)

MUCH ADO ABOUT NOTHING, William Shakespeare. (0-486-28272-4)

FIVE GREAT COMEDIES: Much Ado About Nothing, Twelfth Night, A Midsummer Night's Dream, As You Like It and The Merry Wives of Windsor, William Shakespeare. (0-486-44086-9)

OTHELLO, William Shakespeare. (0-486-29097-2)

AS YOU LIKE IT, William Shakespeare. (0-486-40432-3)

ROMEO AND JULIET, William Shakespeare. (0-486-27557-4)

A MIDSUMMER NIGHT'S DREAM, William Shakespeare. (0-486-27067-X)

THE MERCHANT OF VENICE, William Shakespeare. (0-486-28492-1)

HAMLET, William Shakespeare. (0-486-27278-8)

RICHARD III, William Shakespeare. (0-486-28747-5)

DOVER · THRIFT · EDITIONS

PLAYS

THE TAMING OF THE SHREW, William Shakespeare. (0-486-29765-9)

MACBETH, William Shakespeare. (0-486-27802-6)

KING LEAR, William Shakespeare. (0-486-28058-6)

FOUR GREAT HISTORIES: Henry IV Part I, Henry IV Part II, Henry V, and Richard III, William Shakespeare. (0-486-44629-8)

THE TEMPEST, William Shakespeare. (0-486-40658-X)

JULIUS CAESAR, William Shakespeare. (0-486-26876-4)

TWELFTH NIGHT; OR, WHAT YOU WILL, William Shakespeare. (0-486-29290-8)

HEARTBREAK HOUSE, George Bernard Shaw. (0-486-29291-6)

PYGMALION, George Bernard Shaw. (0-486-28222-8)

ARMS AND THE MAN, George Bernard Shaw. (0-486-26476-9)

OEDIPUS REX, Sophocles. (0-486-26877-2)

ANTIGONE, Sophocles. (0-486-27804-2)

FIVE GREAT GREEK TRAGEDIES, Sophocles, Euripides and Aeschylus. (0-486-43620-9)

THE FATHER, August Strindberg. (0-486-43217-3)

THE PLAYBOY OF THE WESTERN WORLD AND RIDERS TO THE SEA, J. M. Synge. (0-486-27562-0)

TWELVE CLASSIC ONE-ACT PLAYS, Edited by Mary Carolyn Waldrep. (0-486-47490-9)

LADY WINDERMERE'S FAN, Oscar Wilde. (0-486-40078-6)

AN IDEAL HUSBAND, Oscar Wilde. (0-486-41423-X)

THE IMPORTANCE OF BEING EARNEST, Oscar Wilde. (0-486-26478-5)